Text and illustrations copyright © 2013 Elwood H. Smith
Published in 2013 by Creative Editions
P.O. Box 227, Mankato, MN 56002 USA
Creative Editions is an imprint of The Creative Company.
Art directed by Rita Marshall
Printed in China
Library of Congress Cataloging-in-Publication Data
Smith, Elwood H., 1941–
I'm not a pig in underpants / written and illustrated by Elwood H. Smith.
Summary: A rhyming story in which a mysterious animal narrator challenges
readers to figure out its identity by explaining which kinds of animal it is not.
ISBN 978-1-56846-229-5
[1. Stories in rhyme. 2. Animals—Fiction. 3. Guessing games—Fiction.
4. Humorous stories.] I. Title. II. Title: I am not a pig in underpants.
PZ8.3.S6498Im 2013
[E]—dc23 2012046310

First edition
9 8 7 6 5 4 3 2 1

I looked in the mirror
when I got up today

And saw that my skin
was all wrinkled and gray.

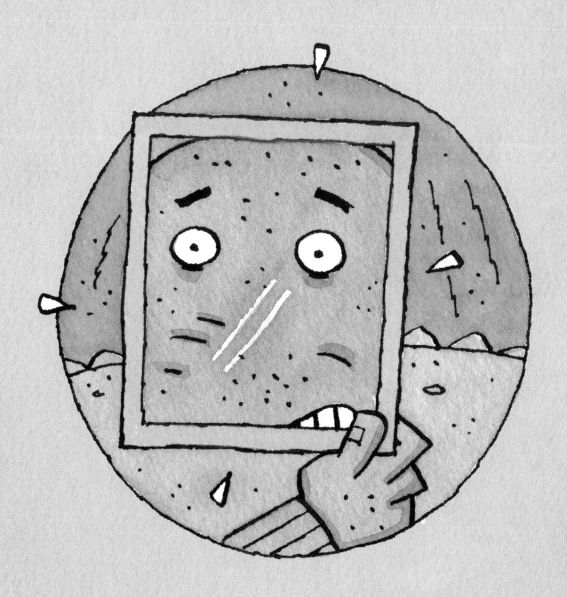

Can you guess what I am? I am counting on you.

Please study each page to discover the clue.

I'm not a tall stork with thin, spindly knees.

Do I live underground? Do I swing in the trees?

I'm not a sad rattlesnake running away.

And I'm not a crocodile playing croquet.

I'm not a round bumblebee trying to buzz.

I'm not a plump platypus watching my weight.

I'll eat every peanut you put on my plate.

I'm not a buzzard invited to France.

NO! I'm not a pig in underpants.

I'm not an orange butterfly using a spoon.

I'm not a brave wolverine on the trapeze.

My ears, you should know,
flap around in the breeze.

I'm not a soft jellyfish crossing the street.

And I'm not a spittlebug keeping the beat.

I'm not a green frog in a flying machine.

And I'm sure not a skunk on a trampoline.

I'm not an odd prairie dog dancing with worms.

Did someone just say I'm a pachyderm?

I look like an elephant, as you can see.

But things are not always what they seem to be.

I spotted a zipper, and to my surprise, I discovered myself:

A small mouse in disguise!

ZIPPER